PUFFIN BOOKS

THE HAUNTED SCHOOLBAG

SMALL GHOST SEEKS
CUMFY HAUNT
NO GOLDFISH
APPLY WITHOUT

'That's an odd sort of sign,' thinks Josh when he notices it on a tree on his way home from school. No one else can see it, and no one else notices when the same small ghost makes his home in Josh's schoolbag. But for Josh, life gets much more complicated. The ghost is determined to do some proper haunting, and that includes clanking, moving things about – even pinching bottoms! Fun for a ghost: big trouble for Josh.

Horace the ghost and his ghost-cat Tinkerbell enjoy a spot of haunting too. When the old rectory where they live is knocked down, they need to find a new home in which to do some floating and moaning. The perfect place is waiting for them somewhere, but how difficult it is to find it! Horace and Tinkerbell discover the world has changed a lot since they last ventured out in 1872.

The Haunted Schoolbag and *Horace the Ghost* are published together in one edition for a double dose of fun. Catherine Sefton is the pen name of Martin Waddell, who has written many books for children. He lives by the sea in Northern Ireland with his wife, three sons and their dog, Bessie.

By the same author

THE GHOST AND BERTIE BOGGIN
BERTIE BOGGIN AND THE GHOST AGAIN!

Catherine Sefton

THE HAUNTED
SCHOOLBAG

Illustrated by Caroline Crossland

PUFFIN BOOKS

PUFFIN BOOKS

Published by the Penguin Group
Penguin Books Ltd, 27 Wrights Lane, London w8 5tz, England
Penguin Books USA Inc., 375 Hudson Street, New York, New York 10014, USA
Penguin Books Australia Ltd, Ringwood, Victoria, Australia
Penguin Books Canada Ltd, 10 Alcorn Avenue, Toronto, Ontario, Canada m4v 3b2
Penguin Books (NZ) Ltd, 182–190 Wairau Road, Auckland 10, New Zealand

Penguin Books Ltd, Registered Offices: Harmondsworth, Middlesex, England

The Haunted Schoolbag first published by Hamish Hamilton Children's Books 1989
Horace the Ghost first published by Hamish Hamilton Children's Books 1991
Published in one volume in Puffin Books 1992
1 3 5 7 9 10 8 6 4 2

Text copyright © Catherine Sefton, 1989, 1991
Illustrations copyright © Caroline Crossland, 1989, 1991
All rights reserved

The moral right of the author has been asserted

Printed in England by Clays Ltd, St Ives plc
Filmset in Baskerville

Contents

The Haunted
Schoolbag

Chapter One

Josh was on his way home from
school when he saw the sign.

It said:

Small ghost seeks
cumfy haunt
No Goldfish
Apply without

Josh stopped and blinked. Then he
read the sign very slowly, twice over,
to see that he had got it right.

The sign was on the old tree at the

end of Cowper's Lane. The sign hadn't been there in the morning when Josh went by on his way to school, and it was only just there now.

It came, and it went, flickeringly. Sometimes it was there, and sometimes it wasn't, all in the same split second.

"Look at that!" he said to Marge.

"What?" said Marge.

"*That*," said Josh, pointing at the sign, which was there when he pointed, but *wasn't* when Marge looked.

"I don't see anything, Josh," said Marge. "Come on, we'll be late for tea."

"But . . ." said Josh.

4

"I'm not hanging about playing
games, little Josh!" said Marge, and
she marched on, leaving her brother
behind her.

"WAIT!" Josh shouted.

"No," said Marge, over her shoulder.

"But . . . but . . . there's a sign on the tree."

"No, there isn't," said Marge. "I've looked, and I *know* there isn't. You're bonkers, Josh!"

And she went off, leaving Josh standing in front of the sign.

He read it again, carefully.

SMALL GHOST SEEKS
CUMFY HAUNT
NO GOLDFISH
APPLY WITHOUT

It should be 'apply within', Josh thought, because he had seen signs

like that before in Mr Shardi's shop
. . . although the signs in Mr
Shardi's shop didn't *come* and *go*, the
way the one on the tree did. Still . . .

"Without *what*?" muttered Josh.
"Goldfish," said the Ghost.
Josh *heard* the word 'goldfish', but
he couldn't *see* anyone.
 "Who said that?" he demanded.
 "I did," said the Ghost.

This time, Josh was sure no one was there.

"A g-g-g-g-g-host!" Josh stuttered.

"But only a small one," said the Ghost. "I'd fit in almost anywhere."

"But . . . but . . ." Josh was scared and interested, all at the same time. He had never met a ghost before, and he wasn't quite certain that he had met one this time, because he couldn't see the ghost. He could only hear it.

"Is that your schoolbag?" asked the Ghost.

"Y-e-s," said Josh uncertainly.

Suddenly his schoolbag gave a wriggle, and a lurch, and banged against his back.

"Right, I'm in," said the Ghost in

a muffled voice from inside the schoolbag. "Very satisfactory, apart from all the crumbs and sweetie papers!"

"I . . . I . . . I . . ." said Josh, grabbing his schoolbag, which gave a sort of wriggle.

"*Careful*," said the Ghost.

"Sorry," said Josh.

"It's time we were going home for tea," said the Ghost. "Mustn't be late, or your mum will be cross."

"J-O-S-H!" Marge yelled, coming back down the lane. "Do hurry up!"

"I told you!" said a muffled voice from the schoolbag.

"Mum's going to skin you alive for mucking about, little Josh," said Marge, and she grabbed Josh and marched him off down the lane.

Bang went the schoolbag on Josh's back.

"Oh!" and "Ouch!" and "Would you believe it!" went the Ghost in the bag, but Marge didn't hear it.

Josh did, but he didn't say anything, because he didn't know what to say.

Chapter Two

"Four places," said Mum, looking at the knives and forks. "And there are only *three* of us. Who laid the table?"

"I didn't!" said Josh.

"I didn't!" said Marge.

"I *did*," said the Ghost, but nobody heard it except Josh.

"You can't count!" said Josh.

"Who can't count?" said Mum.

"Whoever laid this table can't count!" said Marge. "And it wasn't *me*!"

"I *can* count," said the Ghost,

sounding hurt. "One for you, Josh,
one for Marge, one for your mum,
and one for me."

"They don't know you're here,"
said Josh.

"Who doesn't know who is here?"
said Mum.

"Er . . . nobody," said Josh,
getting confused.

"That's right," said the Ghost
cheerfully. "No Body!"

12

It was meant to be a joke, but Josh didn't laugh, because he was beginning to realise that the Ghost was a problem.

Mum sat down, and Josh sat down, and the Ghost sat down, and Marge sat down on the Ghost.

"Ouch!" went Marge, in the middle of sitting *down*, and she shot *up* again suddenly, and almost knocked the table over.

"Marge!' said Mum.

"Somebody pinched my bottom!" said Marge, going red.

"Sit down at once and don't tell lies, Marge," said Mum. "Nobody pinched your bottom. There's nobody there."

"*Exactly*," said the Ghost, floating round to the seat next to Josh, and getting ready to tuck in.

For a small Ghost with no body, it tucked in rather a lot.

"I've never seen you two eat such a tea!" said Mum, when they'd finished. "All that food! I can't think where you put it."

"Neither can I," said Josh.

"Ahem!" coughed the Ghost politely.

14

After tea, Josh and Mum did the dishes and Marge walked the dog.

The ghost went with her. The dog always enjoyed a walk after tea, but this time it didn't.

It kept sniffing and snuffling around, and annoying Marge, who couldn't see what it was sniffing and snuffling at.

The dog (which was called 'Dog') had a very worried walk, and came back home still snuffling, although it stopped when the Ghost slipped off into Josh's schoolbag.

Josh began to think that the Ghost had gone, as mysteriously as it had come . . . or maybe he'd imagined it all.

But he was wrong.

The Ghost was busy, inside the schoolbag, getting organised.

First it threw out all the old sweetie papers and crumbs, which it neatly parcelled up in a page from Josh's jotter, and put in the bin.

The Ghost wrote out two signs, very carefully. One said, 'Private – Keep Out' and the other said,

'Resting – Do Not Disturb'. The
Ghost stuck them on the schoolbag,
one above the other.

Then it made a sleeping bag from
Josh's pencil case and climbed in and
went to sleep, because it had had a
busy day house-hunting.

Chapter Three

It was midnight when Josh woke up.

He didn't usually wake up at midnight. He was usually fast asleep until getting-up time, but *something* wakened him.

It was a sound.

A very small sound

coming from the hall.

Burglars, thought Josh, and he
wondered what to do. Then . . .

Tinkle   Tinkle   Tinkle

and

Tinkle
Tinkle
Tinkle

SPLOSH!

came from the kitchen and somebody
yelled

ooooo OAAAH !

in a very small voice which made Josh realise that it wasn't burglars at all. It was the Ghost.

I'd better go and see what has happened to it, thought Josh, and he climbed out of bed, and padded into the kitchen.

The Ghost was standing next to Dog's dish, dripping onto the tiles.

"Who put that dish there?" it said angrily.

"Mum did," said Josh. "She always puts water out for Dog at night."

"Nobody told me!" grumbled the Ghost, but it wasn't making a joke about No Body, because it was all wet, and cold, and shivery after falling into Dog's dish, and it wasn't in a jokey mood.

Josh couldn't see it, but he could see the drips.

"So much for *clanking*!" said the Ghost.

"Clanking?" said Josh.

"Clanking," said the Ghost firmly. "That's what ghosts do. Clank-clank-clank, like this."

And it went

round Dog's dish.

"That sounds like a tinkle to me," said Josh reasonably, because it did.

"It may sound like a tinkle to you, but it is a clank," said the Ghost. "I'm rather proud of my clanks, considering I can only manage a very small chain."

Josh thought for a bit. "Why can you only manage a very small chain?" he said.

"Because I'm only a very small ghost," said the Ghost, and it tinkled softly off to the bathroom, to dry itself on a towel.

"JOSH?" said Mum. "Josh, what are you doing up at this hour?"

"Er . . . nothing," said Josh. "I just woke up."

"Back to bed, N-O-W," said Mum.

"I'm going to have trouble with this Ghost," Josh muttered and he went back to bed.

Chapter Four

There was no sign of the Ghost in the
morning, but Josh knew it was still
there, because he could see the

Resting – Do Not Disturb

sign flickering beneath the

Private – Keep Out

sign on his schoolbag in the hall.
   The Ghost was recovering from
the effects of its dip in Dog's dish.

It didn't show up until mid-morning and when it did show up it *didn't*, because of course nobody could see it, because it was that sort of ghost. Josh knew that it was there when it sat down in front of the television and asked, "Anything good on?"

"There's a programme about sharks," said Josh.

"Sharks?" said the Ghost. "I don't like programmes about sharks."

"Why not?" said Josh.

"I was swallowed by a goldfish once," said the Ghost.

"What's that got to do with sharks? Sharks are nothing like goldfish," said Josh.

"They are from the inside," said the Ghost with a shudder.

Josh switched off the TV.

"About this Haunt," said the Ghost.

"What Haunt?" said Josh.

"The Haunt I'm here to do," said the Ghost. "In return for board and lodging in your schoolbag. Haunting is what ghosts are *for*, you know. Now, what sort of Haunt had you in mind?"

"Er . . . what sorts are there?" asked Josh, because he wasn't sure if he wanted to be haunted at all.

"Well, there's clanking of course," said the Ghost, and it paused hopefully. "I'm rather good at clanking. I usually clank but . . ."

"No clanking," said Josh.

"I can move things about," said the Ghost. "That can be very scary," and it picked up the flower vase and floated it round the room.

"Put it down!" yelled Josh, because his mum was very particular about her flower vase.

"I take it that moving things is

out," said the Ghost. "In that case I could *moan*."

"I don't think your moaning would be any better than your clanking," said Josh. "That is, I don't think Mum would like it. Clanking, that is, or moaning, or flower vase moving . . ."

"How about rattling bones?" said the Ghost.

"Have you got any?" said Josh.

"I could get some," said the Ghost.

"I don't think Mum would like rattling bones," said Josh. "I don't think Mum would really like being haunted at all."

There was a long silence, followed by a sad sniff.

"In that case, I'd better go," said the Ghost.

"But . . . but . . ."

"I can't stay where I'm not wanted," said the Ghost, its voice floating back toward Josh as it went out through the door.

"Ghost! Ghost! Hold on a minute, I've got an idea!" shouted Josh.

But the Ghost was . . .

. . . GONE.

Chapter Five

"Josh has gone mad, Mum," said
Marge.

"What?" said Mum.

"He keeps talking to his
schoolbag," said Marge.

"Don't be silly, Marge," said
Mum.

"I'm not," said Marge. "Josh is.
Imagine talking to a schoolbag."

Marge went out to the front of the
house.

Five minutes later Marge came
back.

"Mum," she said. "Josh is walking
up and down the lane with an old
chain, clanking it."

"I expect he is pretending he's a
train," said Mum.

"I *expect* he's bonkers," said
Marge.

But Josh wasn't bonkers. He was Ghost-hunting. He wasn't sure how to Ghost-hunt, and the only thing he could think of was to clank up and down the lane, and hope the Ghost would hear him.

He did a lot of clanking, but the Ghost didn't turn up. Josh felt very lonely without his Ghost.

"Mum!" said Marge.

"Yes, Marge?"

"Josh has started talking to trees," said Marge, standing at the gate, and looking down the lane at Josh.

Mum didn't say anything: she was fed up with Marge's stories, but not as fed up as Josh was, talking to a Ghost he was sure was there, and getting no answer.

Then . . .

"I'm getting cross, Ghost!" he shouted at the tree. "I know you're there . . . aren't you?"

"No," said a voice.

"It's you! It's you! I knew you were there."

"It isn't me," said the Ghost, very cunningly. "It isn't me. It is just Another Ghost that sounds like me."

"I see," said Josh, considering it.

"This Other Ghost has come back to tell you that I won't be haunting you anymore, because there's no proper haunting work to do at your house," said the Ghost. "No clanking, no vase lifting, no bone rattling, no moaning, no nothing."

"But there is *something*," Josh said slowly. "If you were here I could tell you all about it."

There was a long silence, and then the Ghost, remembering how comfortable Josh's schoolbag had been, and how warm and cosy it had felt in the pencil case sleeping bag, said carefully, "Tell the Other Ghost about it, and the Other Ghost can tell me."

"I've . . . er . . . thought up a Haunt, Other Ghost," said Josh.

"What sort?" said the voice.

"Er . . . *helpful* haunting. That's it!" said Josh.

"Hmmm," said the Ghost.

"You could . . . you could help me with my homework," said Josh. "And you could do things round the house."

"What things?" said the Ghost. "Clanking?"

"A little clanking, when there's nobody there but you and me," said Josh. "And . . . and . . . you could walk Dog."

"Ghosts don't walk dogs," said the Ghost grandly.

"All right, no dog walking," said Josh.

"Ghosts have their pride, you know," said the Ghost, sniffily. "Ghosts don't go back to houses where they are not needed."

"But you *are* needed," Josh burst out. "*I need you*. I need you so that I'll have someone to play with who isn't rotten Marge. Please, Ghost?"

There was a pause, while the Ghost thought about it.

"It is the *Other* Ghost you're talking to," said the Ghost carefully.

"Get the *Other* Ghost to tell you all about it," said Josh.

"I'll go and see if I can find me," said the Ghost.

Josh put his schoolbag on the ground, with the top flap open.

He waited and waited and waited and . . .

. . . *flap* went the schoolbag
and . . .

"Right, I'm in!" said the Ghost.

They went back to Josh's house
and Josh hung the schoolbag up in
the hall.

The Ghost got busy.

It wrote:

Private – Keep Out

on a sign which it stuck on top of the
schoolbag and then it wrote:

Resting – Do Not Disturb

on a sign which it stuck just below
the Private – Keep Out sign.

And then it hopped back into its
pencil case sleeping bag . . .

. . . and then it had another idea. It hopped out of the sleeping bag and wrote another sign

which it stuck right on the front of the schoolbag.

"Dunroamin?" said Josh. "What does that mean?"

"It's short for DONE ROAMING," the Ghost said. "It's the name I'm calling my house. It means I'm staying here forever!"

And the Ghost did.

Horace the Ghost

Chapter One

One day Horace the Ghost was in the library of the Haunted Rectory, gently stroking his purry Ghost-cat Tinkerbell when . . .

BANG!

Something whacked against the wall. The whole building shook and . . .

CRASH!

A big iron ball swinging from a chain came through the window and

the wall around it, sending bricks and
glass flying everywhere and . . . creak!
BOOOOOOOOOOOOOOM!
The ceiling started to fall and the
whole house fell down!

"H-E-L-P!" squeaked Horace.

The bricks and beams and plaster
didn't hurt Horace and Tinkerbell,
because they were Ghosts. They

floated up through the pile, and settled rather unsteadily on top.

"Oooooooooooh!" moaned Horace, checking to see that all his ghostly bits were in place.

"Hiss!" went Tinkerbell at the man with the crane, who was swinging his big iron ball against the last bit of Rectory wall left standing.

C-R-A-S-H!

Down came the wall, all over Horace and Tinkerbell!

"Who did that?" Horace howled, poking his head up through a pile of bricks and dust for the second time.

"*He* did!" said Tinkerbell, pointing a paw at the crane man with his ball and chain. It should have been a *black* paw, because Tinkerbell was a black cat, but now it was a tabby paw, because of all the dust that had settled on her coat.

"Right!" bawled Horace, and the next moment he whooshed across the Rectory garden past the big sign saying:

DANGER !
DEMOLITION WORK
IN PROGRESS
NO UNAUTHORISED
PERSONS ALLOWED
ON THIS SITE.

and headed straight for the crane
man.

Horace waded in, throwing straight
lefts and rights and haymakers and
dancing about in between with his
fists up shouting, "Take that! And
that! And that!"

"The crane man is still standing," Tinkerbell pointed out.

"Eh?" said Horace.

"I think *you've* been wasting *our* time," said Tinkerbell, who was a sensible Ghost-cat, and didn't believe in punching people, whether or not they believed in Ghosts.

Believing makes a *difference*.

The crane man knew for absolute certain sure that Ghosts aren't, and therefore he didn't believe he was being thumped, banged, smashed, crashed and walloped. If he had believed in Ghosts he might have felt something, because Horace was very cross, but even then it wouldn't have been very much. Invisible arms don't carry much punch-power.

"We should be looking for somewhere new to live," Tinkerbell pointed out.

"But . . . but I like it here!" said Horace.

"You liked it here," said Tinkerbell. "But now here is gone."

"We'll have to find a new haunt!" groaned Horace.

Together they drifted over the rubble and out through the place where the Rectory railings had once been, onto the road.

Chapter Two

The two Ghosts came wisping out of
the Rectory gates. Traffic roared all
around them. As it passed, it blew

Horace and Tinkerbell right onto the
traffic island in the middle of the
Gothering Road. It would have blown
them right off it as well, if Horace
hadn't grabbed onto one of the traffic
signs.

ZOOM!
VAROOOOM!
SWISH!
HONK-HONK-HONK!

Horace clung to the traffic sign,
and Tinkerbell hooked her claws in
the leg of Horace's trousers. Ghosts
are gossamer-light, they weigh almost
nothing, and they knew that the
slightest puff would lift them off the
island into the path of *those*.

Those were the carriages.

The carriages weren't like the

carriages Horace and Tinkerbell had
seen when they were last out of the
Rectory in 1872. The carriages then
were drawn by horses and went clip-
clopping gently by.

"No-no-no horses!" stuttered
Horace.

"There *must* be!" said Tinkerbell.

"There *aren't*!" said Horace.

And there *weren't*.

The strange, horseless carriages
whizzed around all by themselves,
making roaring noises and changing
direction, with their wheels spinning
like mad and their horns honking
angrily.

"Oh! Oh! Oh!" moaned Horace,
sinking down on the dusty grass.

"It's not as bad as all that," said

Tinkerbell, not at all sure that it
wasn't, because the horseless
carriages were pretty terrifying.
Tinkerbell *said* it wasn't too bad
because she knew Horace. Horace
was a timid-type Ghost, and if he got
really scared they might be stuck on
the traffic island forever.

"Yes it is! Yes it is!" moaned
Horace, who was expecting to be run
over any minute.

"Be brave, Horace!" said

Tinkerbell, frisking her tail.

"Woe is me! Woe is me!" wailed Horace. It was one of his Ghost-remarks, the sort of thing he said to people who believed in Ghosts and happened to meet him in the corridors of the Rectory. Usually, it made people jump, but Tinkerbell didn't stir a whisker. She was used to Ghosts, being one herself.

Tinkerbell twitched her tail and decided to take over.

"We've got to get off this *thing*," she said, meaning the traffic island.

"I'm not drifting out in the middle of that," said Horace. "And if we don't drift, how can we get away?"

"We wait for a slow-moving one, and jump on!" said Tinkerbell.

"There aren't any slow-moving ones!" Horace pointed out, as two container lorries flashed by, forcing him to grab onto the traffic sign again.

"There will be, eventually," said Tinkerbell.

And there was.

Chapter Three

Jingle-jangle-jingle.

Arnold Morrison, the demon
milkman, sped by on his milk-float.
Arnold was speeding because he
wasn't supposed to be on the
Gothering Road, but it was the
shortest cut from where-he-was to
where-he-wanted-to-be, and Arnold
was cheating.

That was why he revved his electric
engine up to go as fast as it could go,
and tore past the traffic island, full

speed, four miles an hour, hoping that he wouldn't meet a policeman.

He didn't meet a policeman.

He met two Ghosts instead, but of course he didn't *see* them, because he didn't believe in Ghosts, and he didn't hear them hopping onto his milk-float because they didn't so much as rattle-a-bottle. If he had seen them he would have been cross, because hopping on milk-floats is a dangerously silly thing to do, except for Ghosts. It isn't dangerous for Ghosts, because they can't fall off and hurt themselves.

Jingle-jangle-jingle.

The milk-float pulled off the Gothering Road and turned into Wellington Avenue where Arnold

slowed down, and the two Ghosts
were able to settle themselves on top
of the milk bottles.

"This is the life, Horace!" said
Tinkerbell, who had managed to get
the top off one bottle, and was
experimenting with a paw dip. She
may have been a Ghost-cat, but she
enjoyed *real* milk.

"Well, I don't think so!" said
Horace, who was used to comfortable

window-seats at the Haunted
Rectory, and found milk bottles
distinctly uncomfortable to sit on,
even for someone with a ghostly-
bottom.

"You're never satisfied!" said
Tinkerbell, licking her paw.

"I should think not!" said Horace
huffily. "I have my standards, you
know."

That was when Arnold Morrison
stopped the milk-float, and as Horace
wasn't holding onto anything, Horace
fell off into a puddle.

"Did you mean to jump?"
Tinkerbell asked, springing lightly off
the float.

Horace didn't say anything. He
just sat there and dripped. It was a

good thing that Arnold Morrison didn't look back. If he had, he would have seen the drips, but not the Ghost they were dripping off, because the drips were real, and the ghost was a Ghost. Horace looked like a tiny shower of rain, spattering the pavement.

"Enjoy your bath?" said Tinkerbell.

Horace said one or two very rude

things about cats, and Ghost-cats in particular, but Tinkerbell didn't pay any attention. She was used to Horace, and at least they had escaped from the traffic island.

Horace started to drift down the pavement. It wasn't his usual drift, it was a kind of drift-with-a-drip-or-two, because of his puddle landing.

"Cats don't land in puddles," Tinkerbell remarked.

"Cats had better look out, or they'll get what's coming to them!" muttered Horace angrily.

"Cats can jump off almost anything, and land safely!" said Tinkerbell.

"GRRRRRRRRRR!" said Horace, through gritted teeth.

"Do you feel like sausages and chips?" asked Tinkerbell innocently.

"Yes!" said Horace. Sausages and chips was his favourite meal. He always felt like it, but he didn't get it very often, being a Ghost.

"You don't look like sausages and chips," said Tinkerbell. "You look like a wet fed-up Ghost!"

That was how Horace came to be chasing Tinkerbell down the street, and that was how Horace managed to run into the dog.

Dogs can't see Ghosts (unless they happen to be dogs who believe in Ghosts) but they can *smell* them.

"Arf! Arf! Arf!" went the dog, and up a tree went Horace. Tinkerbell was already up it because, being a

cat, she could spot a dog coming a
mile away.

"H-e-l-p!" gasped Horace.

The dog circled the tree, sniffing
suspiciously. Then it barked
hopefully, and nothing happened.
Then it gave up, and went away.

"This will never do!" said Horace.
"I'm too old a Ghost to run around
like this. I need a nice new haunt!"

"What sort of haunt?" asked
Tinkerbell.

"Somewhere . . . somewhere
Ghost-suitable," said Horace.

"Somewhere where I can rest my old bones."

"You haven't got any bones," Tinkerbell pointed out. "You're a Ghost. Ghosts don't have bones. They have . . ."

"I know what Ghosts have!" growled Horace.

Tinkerbell didn't say anything else. She was a smart Ghost-cat. She knew when an upset Ghost had had enough catty remarks.

Tinkerbell hopped down from the tree neatly.

Horace hopped off the tree.

SPLATT!

Tinkerbell could have said something about cat-landings and splatt-landings, but she didn't. She

66

waited until Horace picked himself up
out of the leaves he had splatted in,
and then she tried to be helpful.

"That looks a nice place to haunt!"
she said, pointing at a house with a
garden and a neat path and gnomes
outside the door.

"Agreed!" said Horace who by this
time would have agreed to almost

anything, and he blew up the path, dropping leaves as he went, like a small whirlwind, only in slow motion.

Horace rang the bell, politely.

Nothing happened.

"Perhaps they're not in?" said Tinkerbell, hopping up on the window-sill.

But they were in. They were sitting round the fire, having their afternoon tea. Three of them, three old ladies.

Two of the old ladies didn't believe in Ghosts, which meant they absolutely couldn't hear Ghost doorbell rings, and the old lady who *did* believe in Ghosts didn't hear the Ghost doorbell ring either. She didn't hear too well and had switched her hearing-aid off because she was bored stiff listening to the other two.

Horace and Tinkerbell drifted sadly away.

It was the same at the next house, and the next, and the next.

"I don't think people believe in Ghosts anymore!" said Horace sadly.

"It's too bad," said Tinkerbell.

"We are doomed to haunt this street forever!" said Horace.

He sat down on the pavement and

gave a big sniff. He would have cried,
but he didn't like Tinkerbell to see
him crying. He may have been a
Ghost, but Horace had his Ghostly-
Pride.

Chapter Four

"I don't know what we're doing here!" Horace said.

They were outside a big building at the far end of Wellington Avenue, looking at a sign which said:

PUBLIC LIBRARY

"Well, I do," said Tinkerbell.

"I suppose it will be warm inside," grumbled Horace, and they went up the steps, where there was another sign.

"What is a vestibule?" Horace asked.

"Don't know and don't care," said Tinkerbell, whisking her tail. "Must be a place for leaving prams in."

"Where do they leave the dogs?" asked Horace anxiously, because he didn't want to meet another dog. But Tinkerbell had already stalked through the door. The door was *shut*, but of course that didn't stop Tinkerbell.

"What about cats?" said Horace, stepping through the door and catching up with Tinkerbell. "It says 'dogs' but I expect it means 'cats' as well."

"Doesn't apply to Ghost-cats!" said Tinkerbell.

"Books!" said Horace, looking round him. "Just like the Rectory Library used to be!" And he sat down in a chair.

He had to get up pretty fast when a fat man sat down on top of him. Ghosts often have that kind of problem with chairs. Horace ended up perched on a window ledge, beside the weekly magazines, where he went to sleep. He had had a bad day, and he needed a little snooze.

Tinkerbell was busy. She was a fast learner. She was working the micro-fiche.

It wasn't difficult to work. She watched some children doing it. There was a folder with shiny films in it. The children picked the subject they wanted, got out the film for it, and popped it into the machine. Then the film showed up in bright letters on the micro-fiche screen. It showed all the titles of books on the subjects they wanted to know about.

Miss Armstrong, the Librarian,

didn't believe in Ghosts, or Ghost-cats for that matter.

She never knew how

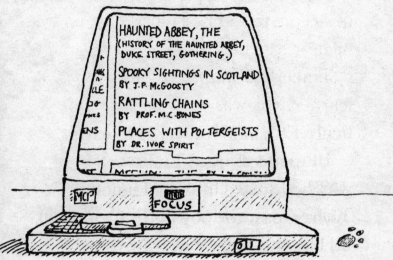

came to be up on the screen, and why there was a paw-print on the desk.

By the time she found it, Horace and Tinkerbell were already on their way to the Haunted Abbey, Gothering, drifting there double-quick to get in before closing-time.

Chapter Five

"NICE!" said Horace. "I like it!"

"Purr-fect!" said Tinkerbell.

They drifted into the Haunted Abbey, past the boy at the Cash Desk, who didn't believe in Ghosts.

"Spooky!" said Horace, with a delicious shiver, and then the man and the lady went by.

"It's a Tourist Trap!" the man said.

"I think it's cheating!" said the woman. "This place isn't haunted."

"Pardon me!" said Horace,
stepping up to them, but of course
they walked right through him, which
isn't especially pleasant for a Ghost.
The man and the woman started
shouting at the Guide.

"But you see . . ." stuttered the
Guide. "There used to be Ghosts . . .
But now no one believes in them, so
no one sees them!"

And the man and the woman went
off, crossly.

"Oh dear!" said the Guide, and he
settled down sadly on a seat, and took
off his Guide-hat. He was tired of
being shouted at by people who said
he made his Ghost stories up.

Then purr-purr-purr.

A cat slipped onto his knee.

The Guide was surprised, but he liked cats, and so he stroked it. His hand went right through the fur he was stroking, but he didn't notice.

"Pardon me," said a voice, from the shadows.

"Sorry sir, we're shut!" said the Guide, putting on his hat and trying to look official. "Probably shut for good. What's the use of a Haunted Abbey, with no Ghosts?"

And then he *looked* . . .

"GHOSTS!" he exclaimed.

"At last!" said Horace. "Someone who believes in us!"

And he drifted into the Abbey Wall, and out of it again, in a little Ghost-dance, to show how pleased he was.

"*Real* Ghosts!" gasped the Guide, and then he looked closer. "But . . . you're not a *monk*. This is an *Abbey*. You're supposed to be a monk."

"I am merely a visitor," said Horace. "A *visiting* Ghost."

"Oh," said the Guide. "That's no good then."

"But you could be a monk, Horace," said Tinkerbell, quickly. "Couldn't you?"

"Could you?" said the Guide.

Horace shimmered, and then he
shut his eyes very tightly and shivered
and changed. One minute he was an
old Haunted Rectory Ghost and the
next he was a monk in a cowl!

"Brilliant!" said the Guide.

"Full-time Haunting, holidays and
weekends extra, but nothing-too-
scary because we aren't scary

Ghosts?" said Tinkerbell.

"Yes! Yes!" cried the Guide.

"And fresh cream and fish daily?" said Tinkerbell. "With sausages and chips for Horace?"

"It's a deal!" cried the Guide.

And that is how the Haunted Abbey at Gothering became the most famous Haunted Abbey in the world,

because it was The-One-With-Real-Ghosts-In-It. People who didn't believe in Ghosts didn't see them, of course, but people who did, *did*.

They saw a monk who drifted round the corridors crying, "Woe-is-me!" and, they saw a purry Ghost who sat around the place, getting fatter and fatter.

"I think I organised that really well!" said Horace.

Tinkerbell had her own ideas about *who* had organised *what*, but she didn't say anything. She just helped herself to more cream, and purred . . .

. . . a soft, ghosty, contented purr.

ADVENTURE ON

SKULL

ISLAND

Tony Bradman

Life for a pirate family is one long adventure!

When Jim finds a treasure map of Skull Island on board the *Saucy Sally*, he knows he and his sister Molly are in for an exciting time. But little do they know that their great enemy, Captain Swagg, is after the same treasure – and is determined to get there first!

NO HOLIDAY FUN FOR SAM

Thelma Lambert

Will Sam have any fun on holiday?

When Sam sees the words NO BUCKETS
AND SPADES IN THE HOUSE in his
hotel, he knows he's in for a dismal
holiday. Kippers for breakfast and
pouring rain...will he ever survive it?
Adding to that, Sam's cub pack plan
to go camping in Wales. Sam is really
excited at the idea, but well-laid plans
can go wrong...

Also in Young Puffin

The Air-Raid Shelter

Jeremy Strong

"Girls first. You go," said Adam.
"But you're the youngest," said
Rachel.
"You're the eldest," said Adam.
They stood there and looked at each
other with set faces.

When Adam and Rachel find an old air-raid shelter they are a little scared of how dark and smelly it seems. But it is the perfect place for a secret camp and with a little work it looks quite cosy...until it is discovered by the bullying Bradley boys.

THE
Friday Parcel

Ann Pilling

**"Look for your parcel. There'll be one
every day, if you're good."**

Matt has to stay on his own with Gran-in-
the-country. To cheer him up, Gran tells
him about the parcels. Each day he
receives a nice surprise, and Friday's is
the best of all.

In the second story, Matt has set his
heart on buying a lion, and the jungle
sale in the church hall sounds just the
place to get one.

MR MAJEIKA
and the
Haunted Hotel

Humphrey Carpenter

Spooks and spectres at the *Green Banana*!

Class Three of St Barty's are off on an
outing to Hadrian's Wall with their
teacher, Mr Majeika (who happens to be
a magician). Stranded in the fog when
the tyres of their coach are mysteriously
punctured, they take refuge in a nearby
hotel called the Green Banana. Soon
some very spooky things start to happen.
Strange lights, ghostly sounds and
vanishing people...